MW01153860

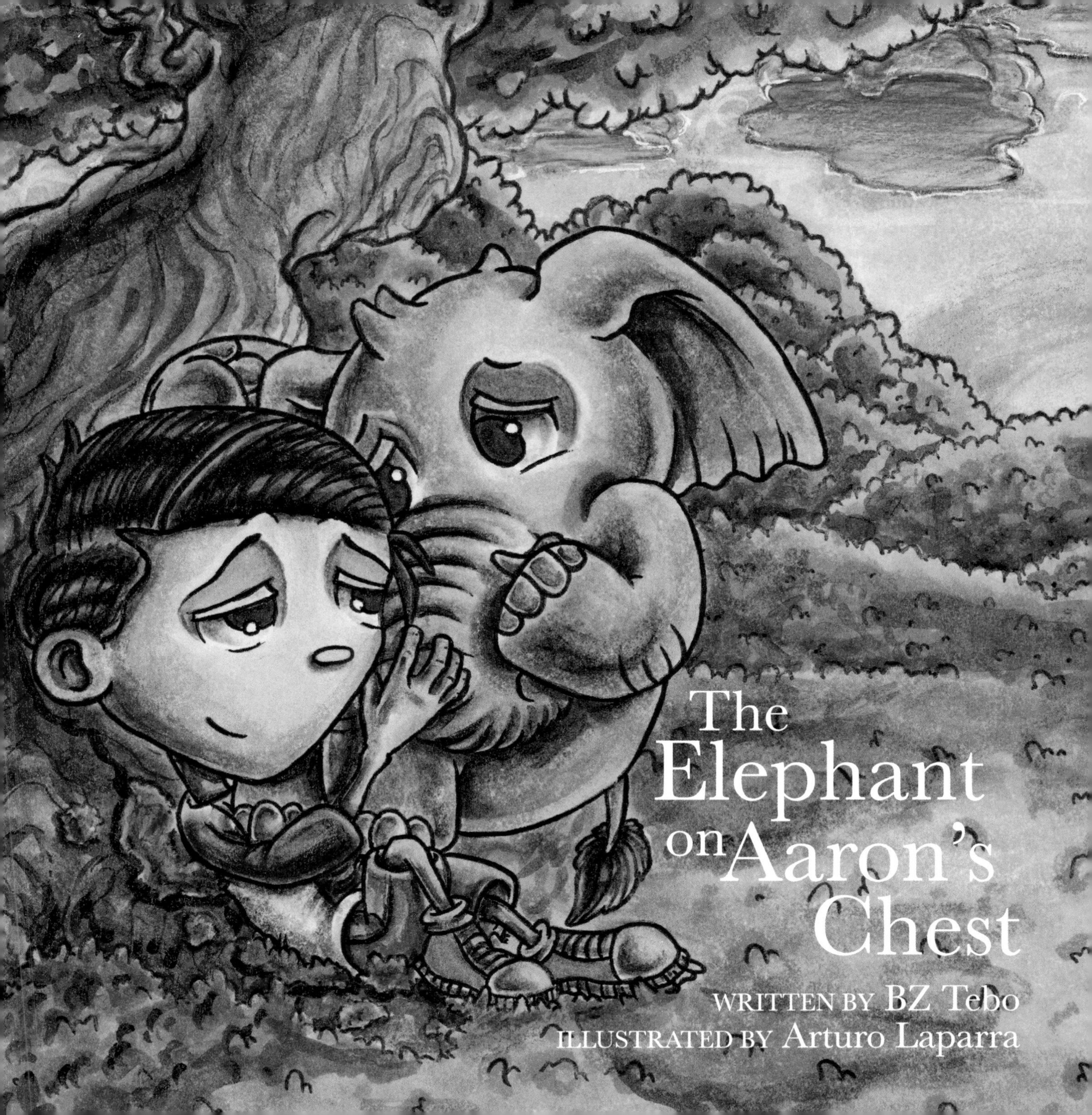

The Elephant on Aaron's Chest

WRITTEN BY BZ Tebo
ILLUSTRATED BY Arturo Laparra

For Shayne and Jaiden. Love lasts forever. - BZ

For my nephew, Maverick. And for anyone struggling with mental health, regardless of age, origin or circumstance. - A.L.

This is Aaron.

This is Aaron's elephant.

Aaron's elephant is sitting on his chest.
The elephant is heavy.

What a silly place for an elephant to be.

It's hard to eat,

It's hard to sleep,

It's hard to play,

When there's an elephant
sitting on you all day.

Aaron tried everything he could think of
to get that elephant to move.

He tried pushing it,

And pulling it.

Scaring it,

And daring it.

He tried tricking it,

And kicking it.

He even tried licking it.

The elephant did not budge.

He poked the elephant.

And pinched the elephant.

He tickled it with a feather.

He wanted to bite the elephant.

And fight the elephant.

He wanted to shove the elephant,
because he did not love the elephant.

The elephant sat.

Aaron cried.

As tears rolled down Aaron's cheeks,
the elephant shifted ever so slightly,
making it easier for Aaron to breathe.

"Thank you," Aaron whispered to the elephant.

The elephant winked.

Aaron began to think.

Aaron reached for his favorite book,
so the elephant could take a look.

Aaron read and read and read.
The elephant listened to every word he said.

Aaron sang the elephant his favorite song.
The elephant sang along.

Aaron went to the kitchen to get a snack.
The elephant moved to Aaron's back.

Aaron picked up his markers to draw.
The elephant liked what he saw.

When Aaron finished his picture, the elephant hopped, well, rather plopped, off of Aaron's back.

Aaron was relieved, but he didn't want the elephant to leave.

He asked the elephant to stay.
The elephant smiled.

Now Aaron can eat,

And sleep,

And play,

With the elephant by his side all day.